The Gingerbread Pirates

For my mother
K. K.

For Molly
M. T.

Text copyright © 2009 by Kristin Kladstrup
Illustrations copyright © 2009 by Matt Tavares

First edition 2009

Library of Congress Cataloging-in-Publication Data

Kladstrup, Kristin.
The gingerbread pirates / Kristin Kladstrup ; illustrated by Matt Tavares. —1st ed.
p. cm.
Summary: When Jim's gingerbread pirate, Captain Cookie, comes alive, the tasty treat prepares to battle
Santa Claus, who likes to eat cookies on Christmas Eve.
ISBN 978-0-7636-3223-6
[1. Cookies—Fiction. 2. Pirates—Fiction. 3. Christmas—Fiction.]
I. Tavares, Matt, ill. II. Title.
PZ7.K6767Gi 2009
[E]—dc22   2007023171

19 20 APS 14 13
Printed in Humen, Dongguan, China

This book was typeset in Erasmus Light.
The illustrations were done in watercolor and gouache.

Candlewick Press
99 Dover Street
Somerville, Massachusetts 02144

visit us at www.candlewick.com

The Gingerbread Pirates

KRISTIN KLADSTRUP   illustrated by MATT TAVARES

CANDLEWICK PRESS

IT WAS CHRISTMAS EVE, and Jim and his mother were making gingerbread men. "Let's make a pirate crew," said Jim. And so they did.

The captain had a gingerbread cutlass and a peg leg made from a toothpick. Jim loved him best of all.

"You'd better leave some pirates out for Santa Claus to eat," said his mother.

"Not Captain Cookie!" said Jim.

At bedtime, Jim took the captain to his room. "I wish you had a ship," he whispered as he climbed into bed. Then he lay awake, listening for reindeer hooves on the roof. Captain Cookie seemed to be listening, too.

Jim fell asleep, but Captain Cookie went on listening.

Where's my crew? he wondered. *And who's this Santa Claus who wants to eat them?* When the house was quiet, he swished his cutlass through the air.

He tested his
peg leg—*tap-step,
tap-step, tap-step.*
He climbed down
into darkness.

Then he ran—
*step-tap,
step-tap,
step-tap.*

He ran until he came to a cliff. He dropped his cutlass over it, then followed. He found his cutlass and then . . .

another cliff!

So he did it all again, one cliff after another, until he reached the bottom. Then Captain Cookie had a shock.

A mouse was nibbling on his cutlass!

"Why, it's half gone!" cried the captain. He grabbed the cutlass and slashed at the air. "Oh, it's ruined!" he moaned, and off he went—*stomp-tap, stomp-tap, stomp-tap.*

"Merry Christmas!" called the mouse.

Christmas! What's that? thought the captain. Then he turned a corner and saw something that astonished him . . .

a huge tree with stars in its branches.

"Ahoy, there!" called a voice.

Looking up, Captain Cookie saw two pirates climbing down toward him. *My crew!* he thought.

The two men—Wavy and Dots by name—dropped to the ground. They jumped right up, but the captain saw that Dots had broken his hand.

No cutlass! And now a wounded man, he thought.

Just then there was a *THUMP.* And a *SCRAPE.* A black cloud puffed toward them.

"Run!" shouted the captain.

They ran until they had to stop for breath.
"Who is that?" asked Dots.

"Must be that cannibal, Santa Claus," said
Captain Cookie. "We've got to get out of here
before he eats us. Where's the rest of the crew?"

"Up on that cliff, I think," said Wavy.

"Start climbing, men!" said the captain.

Up they went. "They're in jail!" cried Dots when they reached the top.

"Save us!" cried the pirates.

Wavy and Dots kicked at the prison walls.

They tried in vain to move the roof.

"What about a rope and pulley from the ship?" said Wavy.

"What about the ship's cannon?" said Dots.

"There is no ship," said the captain. Then he noticed a strange look on Wavy's face, and he whirled around. What he saw made him wish for his cutlass.

A gigantic man was leaning over them. "Young Jim always leaves cookies for me," he said. "But the plate was empty, so I came in here."

"Look out, boys!" ordered the captain.

The big man lifted the prison roof and peered in.

"Don't you eat my crew!" shouted the captain,
raising his fists.

The big man blinked. "This is your crew?" he said.

"Yes," said the captain. "And who are you?"

"I am Santa Claus. And I swear by my sleigh I won't eat your men!"

"Sleigh? What's that? Some kind of ship?"

"That's right."

Swears by his ship—can't be all bad, thought the captain. Still, he was suspicious.

"What are you doing here?" he asked.

"Why, it's Christmas!"

"*Christmas,*" said Captain Cookie. "I wish somebody would tell me what that is."

Santa Claus laughed. "Follow me," he said. "I'll show you a bit of Christmas."

Back beside the starlit tree, the pirates watched as Santa Claus reached into an enormous bag.

"What have you got there?" the captain began.

"It's a ship!" Wavy shouted, and the next thing Captain Cookie knew, his men were swarming its decks and rigging.

"There's cannons! And cutlasses!" cried Dots.

The sky glittered with stars. The captain rubbed his eyes. *Real pirates*, he thought, *and a real ship.* He turned to look back. "Merry Christmas!" he called. But Santa Claus was already gone.

On Christmas morning, Jim's mother found an empty plate on the mantel. "It looks like Santa Claus found the gingerbread men," she said.

But Jim was admiring his presents. His favorite was the pirate ship and its pirate crew.

The captain had a cutlass and a peg leg, and Jim loved him best of all.